Call Me
JONATHAN
for Short

by Cecile Godreau, M.M.

illustrated by
Mary Joseph Peterson, F.S.P.

St. Paul Books & Media

Cover illustrated by Sr. Mary Joseph Peterson, F.S.P.

ISBN 0-8198-1463-6

Printed and published in the U.S.A. by St. Paul Books & Media
50 St. Paul's Avenue, Boston, MA, 02130

St. Paul Books & Media is the publishing house of the Daughters of
St. Paul, an international congregation of women religious serving the
Church with the communications media.

1 2 3 4 5 6 7 8 9   99 98 97 96 95 94 93 92

For Rob, Jonathan and Michael Keating
who taught me to enjoy
the surprises of life.

Contents

Chapter One
A Friend

School was over, so Jay burst out of his fourth grade classroom. Boys were darting in and out, pushing each other happily. He wished he could stay at school a little longer. That's where his friends were and they could play touch football or just chase around and yell at each other. Here, at least, there would be others around. An empty house was no fun to go home to. He checked to make sure he still had his house key.

Jay strolled along the sidewalk, rattling his pencil against each picket of Mrs. Byrne's fence. "Here, young man! Stop that!" Jay listened as the old lady scolded.

A dog leapt up, trying to catch the noisy pencil. Jay jumped back. Then slowly, quietly, Jay's sad blue eyes blinked at Mrs. Byrne through his large glasses.

The old woman's face was painted with lipstick and rouge. But, thought Jay, I can still see how wrinkled she is. She's old, he decided. Old and grumpy, too. Must be a hundred years old, his thoughts continued. And she never seems very happy. I sure don't like her.

"What's the matter with you, boy?" Mrs. Byrne shouted, looking over the fence at him.

Jay scratched the fence with his house key: "JL" for Jay Long. Then he looked up at Mrs. Byrne. It was always the same, he said to himself. Next she would say, "Go home or I'll tell your mother."

"What are you doing to my fence?"

Jay was surprised. He held his key up, and suddenly the woman's voice became soft. "Are you home alone?" she asked. "Isn't anyone at home in your house? Well, why don't you come in and stop making all this racket."

Jay could hardly believe what he had heard. He gathered his books and lunch box, and then walked through the gate and up the path. When he came to the garden, he stopped and watched as Mrs. Byrne began digging again in the plant bed.

"What's your dog's name?" Jay asked, pointing at the red-brown cocker spaniel.

"Name's Penny. Go ahead and call her," Mrs. Byrne waved at the dog. "She won't hurt you."

"Here, Penny," Jay said softly. "Come."

Penny came very carefully, and before long was trying to lick his face. Jay laughed.

"Sometimes she thinks she's a watchdog," Mrs. Byrne explained. "But then she forgets and gets too friendly. She'll be a good friend. In no time at all you'll be playing together— you'll see."

"What are you planting?" Jay asked, putting his arm around Penny's neck.

"Bulbs. They go into the ground before the cold." Mrs. Byrne put her wrinkled hand into a bag. "Here's a tulip bulb. October is the time for them to go into the ground. That's why I'm planting them now."

Jay knew October was bulb planting time. He just wondered why they had to go in

before winter. So he asked Mrs. Byrne, just to be friendly.

"Well," Mrs. Byrne answered, "I never thought about why. It's just that some plants stay in the ground for the winter." She looked up at Jay, who was standing near her. "Do you like to plant?" she asked, her wrinkles making funny lines, while hairs stood out on her chin. Long, white hairs. Jay was fascinated. "Want to help?"

"Yes, ma'am," he said, trying not to watch her chin.

Mrs. Byrne put her bulbs in. "They need a bit of bone meal to grow, so shake a bit into the holes before setting the bulbs in." Jay watched as she showed him.

"Here, boy," Mrs. Byrne said, "take these bulbs and dig holes for them. Don't forget the bone meal and the water." Jay stopped petting Penny and took some of the digging tools.

He worked until he had planted six or seven bulbs. Jay tried to do everything very carefully. Penny wanted to help, and the dog's antics made the boy laugh and laugh.

"She likes you," Mrs. Byrne said. She continued, "This will be your garden, boy. What's your name, anyway?" she asked him suddenly.

"Jay," he answered. "My real name's Jonathan, but they call me Jay for short."

"Well, I'll call you Jonathan for short," Mrs. Byrne grumbled. "Imagine spoiling a perfectly good name. When's your mother getting home, Jonathan?"

Jay wondered why Mrs. Byrne had stopped digging. "Five o'clock," he told her.

"Then you'd better scoot, it's getting dark. Your mother will be looking for you."

Jay said goodbye. He scratched Penny's ears a bit so that she would remember him. Then he ran home. It was just past five, and Mom was taking the groceries out of big bags.

"Where have you been, Jay? You're late. You know you're supposed to come right home."

Jay turned the TV on. "I helped old lady Byrne plant bulbs in her garden."

"Jay!" Mother sounded angry. "Have you been bothering that poor woman? And you're not to call her, 'old lady Byrne.'"

Jay looked at his mother over his glasses. "She showed me how to plant bulbs," he explained. "Did you know she had whiskers?"

Mother frowned at him. "I hope you didn't tell her that."

"Naw," Jay sighed. "And her makeup doesn't hide the wrinkles either."

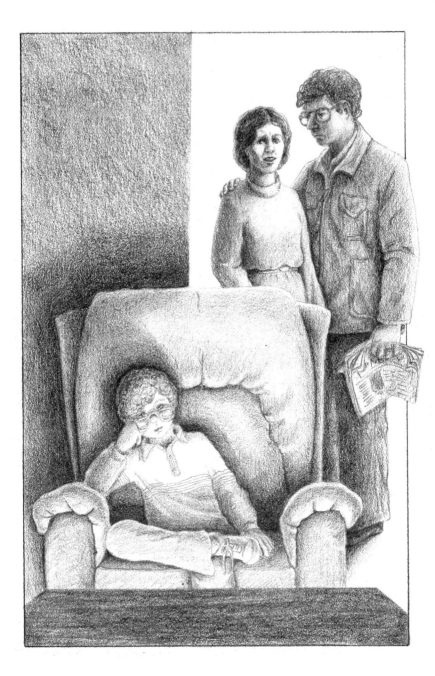

His mother said seriously, "Be kind to her, Jay. She has enough troubles without the neighborhood children giving her a hard time."

"Sure, Mom. I'll try to help."

Dad came home soon after, and Jay could hear his mother telling him about Mrs. Byrne. He watched his dad come into the room. "Jay," Dad said as he dropped his newspaper and removed his coat. He looked so tired. "Your mother and I don't want you bothering Mrs. Byrne, son."

"Yes, sir," Jay said, as he tried to scrape the dirt off his hands.

"Go and wash up," Dad told him. "Supper's ready. And change your pants. They're muddy."

Jay peeled the large pieces of mud off his pants and dropped them into the trash can. Mom hadn't even noticed that his school pants had muddy knees. Maybe he'd better comb his hair, too. He thought about it but decided not to. One time the comb had tangled his mass of curly hair into copper-colored knots. He hated his curls.

Jay wondered if his bulbs were all right; the mud had seemed so cold. Then he joined his parents for supper. That night they were having his favorites: ham and sweet potatoes.

Supper smelled so good! Jay studied his mom's face. She had few wrinkles. And she had no whiskers. How young she was!

"How old is Mrs. Byrne?" Jay asked, making sure to say "Mrs. Byrne" nice and clear.

"She's about eighty, Jay. That's why you're to be good to her," Mom said.

"Yes, ma'am," Jay answered. He didn't mind being good to Mrs. Byrne since she had been so nice to him this afternoon.

Chapter Two
Fall Leaves

The next day at school, Jay watched the trees blowing in the wind outside the classroom window. It was the last week of October and outside was a mass of bright colors. The ground was beautiful where leaves had made mounds of yellow, red and orange. Many more leaves had fallen during the night. Jay felt happy. There would be piles of leaves for him to walk through on his way home.

"Jay," the teacher called him back from his thoughts. She motioned to him to look at his paper. "There will be plenty of time to play later. Now is the time for work, young man."

Jay went back to work. He wanted the day to go faster. Often, he glanced at the clock—only to make sure it was still moving, of course. Now and then he peeked up from his book at the colored leaves outside. How happy he would be to jump into them right now.

At last school was over, and Jay was out the door like a new colt let out to pasture. He had been ready for hours!

Leaves were swirling about in the school yard and tumbling over one another to form heaps. Jay leapt into the leaves. He hid under them and threw them into the wind with both hands. The air was alive with leaves having fun with a happy boy. Jay rolled over and over until he heard his name called.

The teacher was telling him to go home.

Jay started for his house. He kicked the leaves in the gutter ahead of him. They made a crisp, crunchy sound. This was lots of fun, he decided.

As he ran toward Mrs. Byrne's house, he remembered his bulbs and wondered about them. There was Mrs. Byrne in her wool hat

and gloves, bundled for the cold. Boots and a big gray coat almost made her disappear.

Out came the pencil from Jay's pocket. Up and down he went, making it rat-a-tat along the fence. Penny barked her happy sound to welcome him.

"The gate's open. Come in and stop that racket, Jonathan Long," Mrs. Byrne scolded.

Jay scrambled inside, petted Penny and went over to his garden.

It was just as he had left it. "Did they freeze? It was cold last night." Jay was breathless.

Mrs. Byrne smiled at him. "Don't worry, the bulbs are all snuggled in the ground tight and ready for the cold. They like it and are wearing their coats. Not like some boys who swing their jackets behind them and catch cold. My lands! But the bulbs need to be in the cold for a while, to grow beautiful for the spring."

"Oh," said Jay, remembering that spring was a long way off. Could he wait? "What d'you think, Penny?" Jay ran his fingers through the dog's fur. "When's spring coming?" Penny licked him playfully. Then she ran off, so he would chase her.

Mrs. Byrne waved her digger in the direction of the south and exclaimed, "When the robins are packing their bags to come back to us, we'll have spring."

Jay laughed at that.

"But, first," she continued, "you'd best go home and get your school clothes off and then come back. I'll have a bunch of things for you to do."

Jay couldn't move fast enough. Even the door was hard to open today. The leaves were forgotten as he ran back to Mrs. Byrne's house. Where was she? Jay ran through the gate. Her shovel, hoe and watering can were there, but Mrs. Byrne was gone.

"In here," he heard her call.

Jay peered through the door. A glass of juice and a piece of bread were set neatly on the table. Mrs. Byrne was sipping tea. Jay stepped inside and climbed onto a tall stool. He watched as the old lady dunked her bread into her tea. She wasn't even making a mess. Jay admired her.

"I thought you were going to plant bulbs," Jay reminded her, as he munched on his bread.

"Just as soon as I've had my tea. Eat up, Jonathan. You're going to need muscle for this job. That's my honey bread—you like it?"

Jay answered by putting another big piece into his mouth. His head bobbed an

enthusiastic "yes." The juice pushed the bread down easily.

Then on went the coats, and the two made their way to the garden. Jay dug in his plot and put more bulbs in. He knew just what to do. Even Penny helped. Then he stopped, looking at the crocus bulbs. They were tiny, old and wrinkled.

"These aren't any good, are they?" he asked.

"Why not?" Mrs. Byrne responded.

Jay was surprised. Not only did Mrs. Byrne dip her bread into her tea, but she also asked why. When Jay was little he had always asked why—about everything, his mom had said.

"They're old and dried up. That's why," Jay answered.

Mrs. Byrne said, "Hm-m-m," and nodded her head, smiling. "You'd think that they were dead, wouldn't you, but they're just right for planting. You'll see. They'll be up smart and fit in the spring, and they'll come along first, just to prove how alive they are."

Jay looked at the bulbs and then at Mrs. Byrne. The bulbs were as wrinkled as she was.

"People die, too," the boy said slowly, "even good people. But my mom said that one day they will rise like Jesus and be beautiful again." Jay stopped short. Maybe it wasn't polite to talk about death with someone as old as Mrs. Byrne.

Mrs. Byrne didn't seem to mind at all.

"That's a happy thought," she said approvingly. "I'll be planted soon and I'll come back some spring as good as new." She chuckled to herself. "People take a bit longer, that's all. Come now, let's get to planting." She kissed the bulbs, just to let them know she cared, then popped them into the holes.

Jay smiled at her and did the same. Together they put all the bulbs in. Tulips here and crocuses there. All around they planted daffodils.

After a while Mrs. Byrne took a big watch out of her pocket. "You'll have to run," she told him. "My watch says five o'clock. Here— wash first."

Jay started home after peeling great hunks of mud off of his jeans onto Mrs. Byrne's garage floor. "It's all right," Mrs. Byrne assured him. "I'll be sweeping anyway."

Jay's shoes were still muddy, so he took them off when he got home. Mrs. Byrne wasn't afraid of mud, but his mother didn't like mud at all.

"Is that you, Jay?" He heard his mother calling. "Where have you been?"

"We planted again," Jay told her. "We got all the tulips and things in."

"Who and where?" Mother stopped to ask.

"Mrs. Byrne's place. We planted bulbs again."

Jay went to change.

"Jay, we're going over to see Mrs. Byrne. You're probably too lively for her," Mother said later that evening.

Dad agreed with her. Both thought that just for Mrs. Byrne's sake they had better ask how she felt about having Jay come to the house.

"I thought you wanted me to be nice to her," Jay reminded his parents. Suppose Mrs. Byrne were to tell them what he did to her fence or about the time he made her bell stick. He had done it just for fun; he hadn't meant any harm.

Mother called Mrs. Byrne right after supper. "Next Monday evening at five sharp?" she asked. "Yes, Mr. Long and Jay will be there, too."

Jay watched his mother as she came back from her call.

"We're invited to have dinner with Mrs. Byrne," Mother said.

Chapter Three

The Dinner

Nearly a whole week later it was Monday.

Jay thought all day about Mrs. Byrne. He was especially quiet in his classroom. When school was over, the teacher called him to her desk.

"Are you feeling well, Jay?" she asked. "You seemed awfully sad today."

"I've just got a problem, that's all." Jay answered. His head hung so low that his glasses slid right to the end of his nose. He

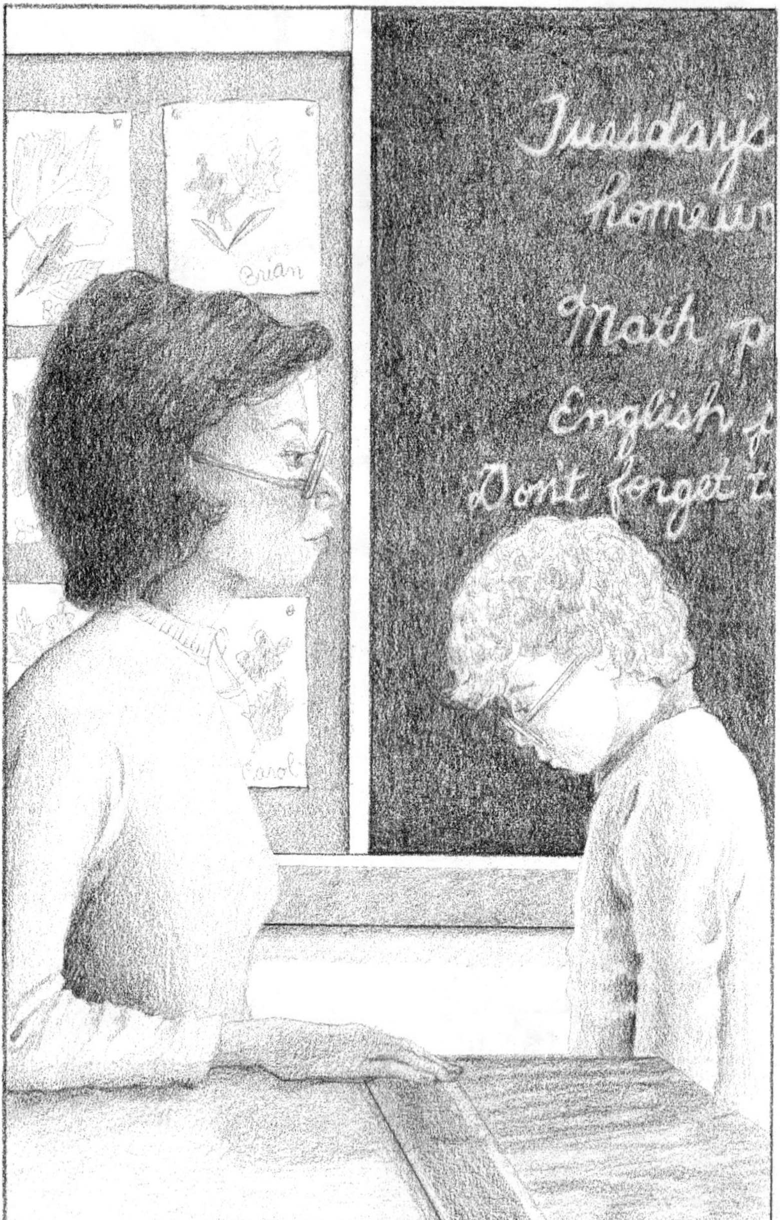
Brian
Carol
Tuesday's
Math
English
Don't forget

really couldn't explain it all. He had always teased Mrs. Byrne and now she was his friend.

He just stood silently, so the teacher told him to go. He turned and started for home. He decided to stop at Mrs. Byrne's house on the way. He thought about the garden and what a good feeling he had when he was there.

The gate was open. He kicked a few stones before going to the door of the house. Penny barked as usual.

"Come in, Jonathan. Help me with the cake. We'll have to crack nuts and get the raisins in."

After everything was done, Mrs. Byrne said, "What's the matter, Jonathan? Don't you feel well? Fine time to be sick."

Jay looked at Mrs. Byrne. "Maybe they won't let me come here anymore. I mean the grown-ups."

"You mean your dad and mother," Mrs. Byrne corrected.

"Yes, ma'am," Jay said softly and sadly.

"Stop worrying and go get ready," Mrs. Byrne assured him. "We'll do fine and dandy."

The three arrived at Mrs. Byrne's house at five o'clock. She had made a delicious dinner. And she had used the beans and alfalfa sprouts that Jay had planted himself. The dinner seemed to be going well.

Penny was in the bedroom because she was bothering everyone.

"She gets bored," Jay explained to his parents. "Penny doesn't really mean to bother. She just wants a little attention, that's all."

"These are great sprouts," Dad told him. "The best I've ever had."

Mrs. Byrne had let Jay crack the nuts and put the raisins into the cake batter and then even bake it. He had also frosted the cake, so he was proud to see desert come in.

Jay felt a bit of happiness coming into him. He had always wanted to help cook. Dad and Mom had their turns, but it never got to be his.

"This was made by Jonathan, too, with a little help from me," Mrs. Byrne told them.

Even Mother's eyebrows arched in pleased surprise. "Why, Jay, I never realized how much you like to cook!"

Then Dad cleared his throat. He was about to say something important.

This was the time Jay had worried about. He watched as his dad spoke to Mrs. Byrne. "You know," he began. "Jay's mother and I are worried. We think that he's probably giving you some problems. We just want you to know that if Jay is bothering you..."

"You want tea?" Mrs. Byrne did not seem to be listening. "This is my own tea. I have my own honey, too."

Dad and Mom took tea. They took the honey, too.

"Now what's that about Jonathan?" Mrs. Byrne asked.

Jay piped up. "They think I'm bothering you. I told them I was helping you plant. I'm sorry I carved my initials on your fence. I'd like to keep coming to your garden." Jay was trying to help Mrs. Byrne decide.

"Well, can you imagine!" she told Jay. "Did you tell them you had a garden, Jonathan? Why, he's been a good help, a little bold at times, but a good help. I think the day he's bold again, I'll just put him out."

"Then I can come?" Jay looked over at Mrs. Byrne.

"Well, I can't figure out why a boy as active as you are wants to visit an old lady. But if it's planting you're wanting, well, this is as good a place as any. I'll teach you more about sprouts, too. And you can help me with the bees any time you like."

Mom didn't like the idea of the bees, so that was put off limits. But Dad promised

that he would buy tools just for him. Jay felt happiness come back into his chest as Mom and Dad thanked Mrs. Byrne. He gave her a big hug.

"That wasn't so hard was it?" she asked him with a wink.

Mother and Dad laughed. They were happy, too.

Chapter Four

Spring

After winter, spring would come to the garden. The days were warmer and the sunshine grew a little stronger. Mrs. Byrne was out again working and digging.

"Spring is here," Jay shouted to her as he neared her house.

"Just about. Come and see," Mrs. Byrne called out. "Look," she said. "They've come!" All over the garden, tiny spikes of green pierced the ground.

"The plants have sprouted," Jay said, getting down on his knees and putting his face close to the green leaves. "There's still snow. They won't catch cold, will they?"

"No, but you will, if you kneel on the ground like that. Here, put some newspaper under you. See the small ones? They're crocuses."

"What are these?" Jay pointed.

"Those are snowdrops. They're the sturdiest of the little flowers. Don't care how much snow's around. They just come marching through."

Each day a bit more color was added to the yard. Crocuses sent up small packages of yellow and purple and white, while daffodils and tulips grew spikes that reached higher and higher. The trees were shouting, "Look at me," and the birds were hopping in to inspect the baby leaves that the branches held at their fingertips.

"Spring has really come," Jay called out one day.

"Yes," laughed Mrs. Byrne. "I think it's here."

Jay saw spring happening all around. The apple trees looked pretty with flowers, and tight knots opened on the dogwood, showering the tree with star-shaped puffs of white and pink that swung back and forth like happy children.

"But," Jay wanted to know, "where are the bees?"

"They've been here all along," Mrs. Byrne told him. "They took everything into the hive for the winter. They'll be getting to work soon."

And that's just what happened next.

"Look," Jay shouted one day. "The bees are out and hunting for flowers to visit."

A robin hopped over to pick up a twig, and a pair of red birds tried the ground for pecking.

"Everybody's back," Jay shouted, and Penny barked.

April and vegetable planting came together. Tomatoes that had been started inside the house were planted outside. Then came the beans and peas and lettuce.

"Do you *have* to plant carrots?" Jay asked.

"You plant your favorites, and I'll plant mine," Mrs. Byrne told him.

Jay thought a while. Tomatoes and lettuce would go into his garden, for sure.

All of April was a busy time with the planting. Penny "worked," too, digging holes here and there. And the bees buzzed all over every day, gathering honey for their new babies. Jay's tomatoes and lettuce sprouted. Everything had come alive again. Jay was happy.

"If you're planted someday, will you come up like all the plants?" Jay asked, studying Mrs. Byrne's face.

"Sort of," she said smiling. "I'll come out like new after I'm planted. Each creature comes in its own time. God knows the best time for each."

"Will I be planted someday?" Jay had never thought of that before.

"Yes," Mrs. Byrne answered. She stopped her digging and looked at the boy. "When you're wrinkled and old, you too will sleep in the ground next to the flowers."

Jay wanted to tell Mrs. Byrne something. "And I'll come back happy, like the spring."

"As happy as a daffodil and probably just as bold. And you'll make everyone as happy as you make them right now."

Jay thought a bit. He was thinking so hard that his father had to call him twice. Only when Mrs. Byrne nudged him did he see his father at the fence.

"Are you coming home?" he heard Dad call.

Jay gathered his tools and ran home with his father. Inside he felt as joyous as all the plants around him.

He had so much to tell the other boys when June came. He was looking forward to seeing David at camp. He would tell him all about the bulbs, and about how someday, after being planted, there would be spring for everybody. That's what resurrection meant. He had known it all along.

Chapter Five

Jonathan

Jay ran as fast as he could to Mrs. Byrne's house. He was going off to camp, and 'goodbyes' had to be said to Mrs. Byrne, to his garden and to Penny. The house was very silent. Where was Penny? Jay tiptoed as softly as possible. Then he heard barking. He stood on the porch waiting and finally gave the door a push. It opened. Penny jumped up, wanting to be patted, so Jay knelt and hugged the happy dog.

"Where's Mrs. Byrne?" Jay asked Penny, as if the dog could answer.

"Over here, Jonathan," Mrs. Byrne called.

Jay followed her voice into the next room. There she sat, looking so small. She had never looked that small to him before. A big shawl covered her shoulders, and her feet were resting on a stool.

"Where you bound for, all washed and shiny?" Mrs. Byrne asked.

Jay plopped onto the floor at her feet. "I'm going to camp, but I came to say goodbye. Hey, you're not sick or something, are you?"

"Nothing my honey and tea won't fix," Mrs. Byrne snapped. Then she went on more softly. "Where's camp? Come and tell me. Penny, let the boy sit closer so's I can hear him."

"Well," Jay began, putting his arm around Penny. "Camp is up in the mountains. I'm spending the summer there. My friend David comes each year and so does Ken. Ken knows almost as much as you do about plants."

"Bosh, no one knows *that* much," Mrs. Byrne pretended to growl.

"It's true! He's everyone's favorite. He knows about scouting and everything. Hey, Mrs. Byrne, don't you feel well? How come you're inside?"

Penny looked at him and then put her head in his lap. She looked very sad.

"Penny's always loved you, Jonathan. I want you to have her if I ever have to go to a hospital or anything."

Jay was surprised when Mrs. Byrne said "hospital." "Are you going to a hospital?" he asked quickly.

"Hospital?" Mrs. Byrne made her eyes open wide. "Who said anything about that? No one will make me go, that's for sure." After a little while she added, "You'd like a dog wouldn't you, Jonathan?"

"You mean Penny?" Jay sat up.

"I guess that's what I had in mind," she confessed. "Well, you think about it. All right?"

"Yes, ma'am." Jay was thrilled! "Wait 'til I tell my parents!"

A horn sounded. Mom was ready to go.

"What about a hug and then you run along, Jonathan. I won't go to the door. Too cold out today."

Jay obliged and then ran out to his mother. "She wants me to have Penny if she ever goes away," he said breathlessly. "May I have her? And, Mom, she cried when I said goodbye."

"She'll miss you, Jay. We'll talk about the dog later. Now let's get to camp. Hurry, or we'll miss your bus."

When he saw Ken, Jay told him about Mrs. Byrne and about the sprouts they had grown together. Ken had him show the boys and had him sprout the tiny seeds he'd brought with him. The boys' eyes were wide with wonder as the long white roots and tiny leaves appeared. They were even more surprised to see them eaten in a sandwich! It had taken only five days of careful watering for the seeds to grow.

Jay told everyone about the wondrous purple and yellow flowers that sprang out of the oldest bulbs anyone had ever seen.

"It's just like the resurrection," he explained. "My friend's really smart. She looks like she's a hundred but she's only eighty years old," Jonathan bragged. "And she keeps bees."

Ken was very pleased and told Jay he should get a medal just for all the things he had learned with his friend.

"She sounds like a great lady," Ken told him.

Soon it was time to say goodbye again. Jay finished packing and got on the bus. His mother met him at the station. They got his bags and went to the car. He would miss all the boys, but he was happy to be going home.

"We've planned a good vacation at the seashore," Mother told him. "Won't that be great?"

Jay agreed. It would be good to be with his parents again.

When they got home, Jay remembered his garden. "May I just go over to see my garden a minute?"

Mother looked very serious. Jay wondered what was wrong.

Mother looked down at Jay and put her hand on his shoulder. "Jay, Mrs. Byrne doesn't live down the street anymore. You see, that hot spell we had made her very weak. Mrs. Byrne was very old. She died, Jay. I think other people are planning to buy the house."

Jay blinked very hard to keep the tears from coming out. He turned toward the house. Then he saw Penny waiting for him on the porch. She cried and yapped with delight.

Jay knelt and hugged the dog, his dog. It's okay, Penny, he thought. I'll take good care of you, I promise. Jay put his face in the

dog's fur. He couldn't believe that Mrs. Byrne wasn't at her garden anymore. "Was she planted?" he asked softly.

Mother looked surprised. "Well, yes. She was buried."

"May I see where they put her?" Jay pushed his glasses up.

"If you want to. We'll go together," Mother answered.

That afternoon, they visited the spot where Mrs. Byrne's body was buried. Penny went, too, on a new leash. She walked close to Jay.

It seemed that the sun was warm and gentle. The sky was happy in a quiet way. And there was soft green grass and colorful flowers. Jay looked at his mother.

"It's okay, Mom, Mrs. Byrne will be happy about being planted here. She's with God now, isn't she? And God knows when she'll bloom again. Just think how happy she'll be when spring happens to her. She told me that it takes a little longer for people, that's all. Someday I'll see her again. I hope she remembers me, Mom."

"I'm sure she does, Jay," Mom said softly.

Jay felt a little sad. He only wished Mrs. Byrne had waited to say goodbye. Why had she been in such a hurry? She had always seemed to tell him to hurry—maybe that was why. He looked back to the place where Mother had shown him Mrs. Byrne's name on a block of stone. Anyway, Jay decided, I feel good about her body being planted in such a beautiful garden.

"Goodbye, Mrs. Byrne," he called as he turned back toward his mother. "Come on, Penny!" The dog jumped and ran ahead of him.

Mother smiled. "Mrs. Byrne is happy, Jay."

"Yeah," Jay said as he ran his fingers through Penny's fur. Then he turned and waved, not at the grave, but somewhere near the sun. "She's waiting for her special spring. She calls resurrection, 'springtime'," he told his mom.

His mother put her arms around his shoulders. "That's nice, isn't it, Jay?" she said smiling.

"Mom." Jay looked serious again. "I'm almost in fifth grade. Would you call me Jonathan from now on, for short?"

"Sure," Mom said, hugging him. "Let's go, Jonathan."

About the Author:

Cecile Godreau, MM, is a Maryknoll Sister. As a missionary in Bolivia for eighteen years, she taught school, led retreats and trained catechists—all in Spanish! In Bolivia, Sister Cecile met many children who had to grow up too fast. She wished they could have had time, like Jonathan did, to enjoy the interesting and fun parts of growing up. "I guess Mrs. Byrne is very much me," she said.

ALASKA

750 West 5th Ave., Anchorage, AK 99501 **907-272-8183.**

CALIFORNIA

3908 Sepulveda Blvd., Culver City, CA 90230 **213-397-8676.**

1570 Fifth Ave. (at Cedar Street), San Diego, CA 92101 **619-232-1442;
619-232-1443.**

46 Geary Street, San Francisco, CA 94108 **415-781-5180.**

FLORIDA

145 S.W. 107th Ave., Miami, FL 33174 **305-559-6715; 305-559-6716.**

HAWAII

1143 Bishop Street, Honolulu, HI 96813 **808-521-2731.**

ILLINOIS

172 North Michigan Ave., Chicago, IL 60601 **312-346-4228;
312-346-3240.**

LOUISIANA

4403 Veterans Memorial Blvd., Metairie, LA 70006 **504-887-7631;
504-887-0113.**

MASSACHUSETTS

50 St. Paul's Ave., Jamaica Plain, Boston, MA 02130 **617-522-8911.**

Rte. 1, 885 Providence Hwy., Dedham, MA 02026 **617-326-5385.**

MISSOURI

9804 Watson Rd., St. Louis, MO 63126 **314-965-3512; 314-965-3571.**

NEW JERSEY

561 U.S. Route 1, Wick Plaza, Edison, NJ 08817 **908-572-1200;
908-572-1201.**

NEW YORK

150 East 52nd Street, New York, NY 10022 **212-754-1110.**

78 Fort Place, Staten Island, NY 10301 **718-447-5071; 718-447-5086.**

OHIO

2105 Ontario Street (at Prospect Ave.), Cleveland, OH 44115
216-621-9427.

PENNSYLVANIA

214 W. DeKalb Pike, King of Prussia, PA 19406 **215-337-1882;
215-337-2077.**

SOUTH CAROLINA

243 King Street, Charleston, SC 29401 **803-577-0175.**

TEXAS

114 Main Plaza, San Antonio, TX 78205 **512-224-8101.**

VIRGINIA

1025 King Street, Alexandria, VA 22314 **703-549-3806.**

CANADA

3022 Dufferin Street, Toronto, Ontario, Canada M6B 3T5 **416-781-9131.**